ZONDERKIDZ

The Berenstain Bears® Treat Others Kindly
Copyright © 2012 by Berenstain Bears, Inc.
Illustrations © 2012 by Berenstain Bears, Inc.

Requests for information should be addressed to:
Zonderkidz, 5300 *Patterson Ave SE, Grand Rapids, Michigan* 49530

Library of Congress Cataloging-in-Publication Data
Berenstain, Jan, 1923–2012.
    [Berenstain Bears, the forgiving tree]
    Berenstain Bears treat others kindly / Jan and Mike Berenstain.
       p. cm. — (Berenstain bears living lights)
    Summary: A misunderstanding on Brother Bear's birthday leads to hurt feelings, but Sister Bear
meets him in their backyard treehouse and reminds him of the importance of forgiveness.
    ISBN 978-0-310-73492-5
    [1. Birthdays—Fiction. 2. Parties—Fiction. 3. Forgiveness—Fiction. 4. Bears—Fiction.
5. Christian life—Fiction.] I. Berenstain, Mike, 1951– II. Title.
PZ.B44826Br 2012
[E]—dc23   2012030228

The Berenstain Bears® Show Some Respect ISBN 9780310720867 (2011)
The Berenstain Bears® Forgiving Tree ISBN 9780310720843 (2010)
The Berenstain Bears® Gossip Gang ISBN 9780310720850 (2011)

All Scripture quotations, unless otherwise indicated, are taken from The Holy Bible, *New International Version®*, *NIV®*. Copyright © 1973, 1978, 1984, 2011 by Biblica, Inc.™ Used by permission. All rights reserved worldwide.

Scripture quotations marked NIrV are taken from The Holy Bible, *New International Reader's Version®*, *NIrV®*. Copyright © 1995, 1996, 1998 by Biblica, Inc.™ Used by permission. All rights reserved worldwide.

Any Internet addresses (websites, blogs, etc.) and telephone numbers in this book are offered as a resource. They are not intended in any way to be or imply an endorsement by Zondervan, nor does Zondervan vouch for the content of these sites and numbers for the life of this book.

Zonderkidz is a trademark of Zondervan.

Editor: Mary Hassinger
Cover and interior design: Cindy Davis

Printed in the United States of America

13 14 15 16 17 18 /DCI/ 13 12 11 10 9 8 7

"For if you forgive other people when they sin against you, your heavenly Father will also forgive you."

—Matthew 6:14

The Berenstain Bears

The FORGIVING TREE

Living Lights™

ZONDERVAN.com/
AUTHORTRACKER
follow your favorite authors

ZONDERkidz

It was a special day in a tree house down a sunny dirt road deep in Bear Country. It was Brother Bear's birthday.

"Happy Birthday, Brother!" shouted the party guests as Mama brought in the cake. Then they all sang the birthday song.

"Make a wish!" said Sister.
Brother closed his eyes, made a wish, and blew out the candles.
"YEA!" the guests yelled, clapping and blowing on noisemakers.

Papa cut the cake and everyone dug in.
"What did you wish for?" asked Cousin Fred.
"If I tell, it won't come true," said Brother.

When they were finished eating the cake, it was time to open presents. Brother got some very nice ones—a model plane, some books, a racing car set, and a video game.

Then he noticed Papa sneaking into the next room. When he came back, he was pushing ... *a brand-new bike!*

"Wow!" said Brother excitedly. "It's exactly what I wished for!"

"Lucky you didn't tell Fred," said Sister.

"That's a beautiful bike," said Fred, admiring it. "I sure wish I had a bike like that."

"Oh," said Brother, without thinking, "you can borrow it anytime you like."

"Gee, thanks!" said Fred.

"Let's try out your new video game," suggested Sister.

All the cubs crowded around while Brother and Sister played the new video game. They were so interested, they didn't notice anything else for awhile. But then Brother looked over at his brand-new bike. It was gone!

"Hey!" said Brother. "Where's my new bike?"

"Say," said Lizzy, looking out the window, "isn't that Fred riding it?"

Lizzy was right. Cousin Fred was outside riding Brother's brand-new bike around the tree house. Brother was furious!

"That Fred!" growled Brother. "He can't do that!" And he
charged outside.
    "Uh-oh!" said Mama and Papa, running after him.

But they were too late. Brother was already chasing Fred around the tree house yelling for him to get off his bike. He startled Fred so much that poor Fred didn't look where he was going and ran right into the mailbox.

He wasn't hurt, but the bike was. The front wheel was bent and wouldn't turn.

"Look what you did!" shouted Brother. "Who said you could ride my new bike?"

"*You* did," said Fred. "You said I could borrow it anytime."

"I didn't mean right away," said Brother, stamping his feet. "I never even got to ride it!"

"Now Brother," said Mama, "calm down. This is just a misunderstanding. Fred didn't mean any harm."

"But my bike is ruined!" cried Brother. "Just look at it!"

"It's not ruined," said Papa. "We'll take it down to the bike shop and get it fixed up as good as new."

"But it won't be new!" said Brother. "It will never be brand-new again!" And he stormed off in a huff.

"Gee, I'm sorry," said Fred. He felt awful. "I never meant to hurt Brother or his new bike."

"Of course not, Fred," soothed Mama. "It was just an accident."

"I'm sorry Brother's so mad," said Fred. "Do you think he'll ever forgive me?"

"Of course he will," said
Papa. "He'll get over it in no
time."

But Sister wasn't so sure.
She followed Brother to
their backyard tree house.

"Mind if I come up?" she called. Brother didn't answer. Sister climbed the ladder and found Brother sitting, sulking, at the top.

"You're certainly in a good mood," said Sister.

"Humph!" grunted Brother.

Sister noticed a faded red line drawn down the middle of the tree house floor.

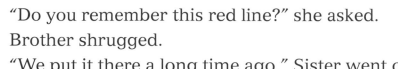

"Do you remember this red line?" she asked.

Brother shrugged.

"We put it there a long time ago," Sister went on. "We were so mad at each other that we divided the tree house in half. I sat on one side, and you sat on the other. We sat out here being mad at each other until it started to rain and we got soaked. By that time, we couldn't even remember what we were mad about."

"I guess so," said Brother.

As Brother and Sister sat in their tree house, it became cloudy and started to rain. They went back to the party and found the guests getting ready to break the piñata.

It was one Papa made in his workshop. There were all kinds of candies inside but especially licorice because licorice was Papa's favorite. Papa held the piñata out on a broomstick.

"Okay," he said. "Start swinging. But be careful not to hit *me*!"

One after another, the cubs whacked the piñata until it finally broke open, spilling candy onto the floor.

They all scrambled to grab some, including Papa. Brother scrambled right into Fred. In fact, they knocked heads.

"Ow!" said Fred, rubbing his noggin.

"Oops, sorry!" said Brother.

"That's okay, Brother," said Fred. "I forgive you."

"I forgive you too, Fred," said Brother, feeling ashamed of himself. "I shouldn't have yelled at you about the bike. It really was just an accident."

"Forget it," said Fred … and forget it they did as they gathered up the candy.

"You know," said Papa to Mama, as they watched the happy cubs, "that old tree in the backyard has seen a lot of forgiving over the years. I guess you'd call it a Forgiving Tree."

"As the Lord said," smiled Mama:
"And forgive us our debts, as we forgive
our debtors."

"What does that mean?" asked Sister.

"Just that God wants us to forgive those who hurt our feelings," said Mama.

"And, remember," added Papa, "though God wants us to be good, he forgives us when we do something wrong."

"Well, I think that's very nice of God," said Sister.
"Yes," agreed Mama and Papa, "it is!"

Activities and Questions from Brother and Sister Bear

Talk about it:

1. Would you have done the same thing as Brother and offered to share your bike with Cousin Fred? Why?

2. Would you have been as upset as Brother if someone that you care about had an accident with something that was yours? What might you do differently?

3. How was Sister a help to Brother?

4. Why is it sometimes very hard to say you are sorry and also hard to accept an apology?

Get out and do it:

1. On a large sheet of butcher paper, design a Family Forgiving Tree. Have an envelope filled with cut-outs of leaves near where you hang the tree. When you need to say you are sorry to someone, write about it on a leaf and tape it to the tree. It feels good to ask for forgiveness and to be forgiven!

"Without wood a fire goes out;
without gossip a quarrel dies down."

—Proverbs 26:20

The Berenstain Bears'
Gossip Gang

written by
Jan & Mike Berenstain

Living Lights™

ZONDERVAN.com/
AUTHORTRACKER
follow your favorite authors

ZONDERkidz

Lizzy and Suzie were Sister Bear's best friends. They liked doing all sorts of things together. They rode bikes and jumped rope.

They played soccer outside and video games inside. They had tea parties with their dolls and stuffed animals. And sometimes they just sat around and talked.

They talked about anything and everything. They talked about TV shows and toys, about games and songs, about pets, parents, brothers and sisters, and, of course, their other friends.

"Did you hear about Queenie?" asked Lizzy. Queenie McBear was an older cub who was very popular. "I heard she has a big crush on Too-Tall Grizzly, but he has a crush on Bonnie Brown!"

"Oooh!" said the others. They were too young to have crushes yet. But they liked to talk about them.

"Did you get a load of that new cub in school?" asked Suzie. "His name is actually Teddy Bear!" The others laughed. Suzie had been a new cub not so long ago. But she didn't seem to remember.

"Well, I saw Anna Bruin the other day," said Sister, "and, you know, I think she put on some weight. She looks sort of chubby."

Lizzy and Suzie giggled.

The three friends talked for a while longer but it was soon dinnertime. "See you!" said Sister, heading home. She liked talking to Lizzy and Suzie about other cubs. It made her feel special and "in-the-know."

Back home, Mama and Papa were setting the table. Brother and Sister joined them.

"Do you know what Herb the mailman told me?" Papa said to Mama as he laid the silverware.

"I can't imagine," said Mama, busy putting out plates.

"He said someone saw Mayor Honeypot throwing a banana peel out his car window. Imagine—the mayor, himself, a litterbug!"

"Now, Papa," said Mama, "you know that's just gossip. You shouldn't spread stories like that."

Papa looked a little ashamed. "I guess you're right. It was just so interesting."

As they sat down to dinner, Sister had a question.

"Mama," she asked, "what's gossip?"

"Well," Mama began, "gossip is when we tell stories about others—especially stories that make them look bad. It's something we do to make ourselves feel special. It can be very hurtful.

"As the Bible says, 'gossip separates close friends.'"

"Oh," said Sister, worried. She thought maybe saying that Anna looked sort of chubby was gossip. She decided not to think about it anymore.

The next day, Sister saw Lizzy and Suzie walking ahead of her on the way to the playground. They were busy talking and didn't notice Sister coming up behind them. As Sister drew near, she overheard them talking … about her!

"Do you know what Anna told me about Sister?" began Lizzy.

"No, what?" asked Suzie, eagerly.

"She saw Sister's spelling quiz when Teacher Jane was handing back the papers, and it was marked, '60%—very poor!'" said Lizzy.

"Wow!" said Suzie.

When Sister heard that, she stopped short. In the first place, it wasn't true. Her quiz was marked "70%—fair." That wasn't too good, but it wasn't as bad as all that.

And, in the second place, why were Lizzy and Suzie gossiping about her? They were supposed to be her best friends. She felt so bad she hid behind a tree until Lizzy and Suzie were out of sight.

As Sister came out from behind the tree, Brother Bear walked by. He was on his way to play catch with Cousin Fred.

"What on earth …?" he said. "Why are you hiding behind a tree?"

"I didn't want Lizzy and Suzie to see me," said Sister.

"Why not?" he asked.

"Because they were gossiping about me and I heard," said Sister. "I was so embarrassed!"

"I'm sorry," said Brother. "Why don't you come along with me and play catch with Fred?"
So they did.

At the playground, they started tossing the ball around. Sister could see Lizzy and Suzie on the swings, nearby. They waved and Sister waved back. Then she got angry.

"You know what I heard about Lizzy?" she called, loudly, to Fred.
"I heard that she is a big silly dope!"

"Huh?" said Fred.

"And you know what I heard about Suzie?" she yelled, even louder. "I heard that she is a funny-faced noodle-brain!"

"Sister!" said Brother.

When Lizzy and Suzie overheard Sister, they jumped off the swings and came charging over.

"Why are you saying bad things about us?" they yelled. "We thought you were our best friend!"

"That's just what I thought!" said Sister. "But I heard you gossiping about me on the way here!"

"Oh," said Lizzy. She hadn't thought about it that way. "I guess you're right. We were gossiping about you. I'm sorry!"

"Me too!" said Suzie.

Sister got over being angry right away. After all, Lizzy and Suzie were her best friends.

"That's okay," she said. "Maybe it would be better if we just didn't gossip about anyone."

Lizzy and Suzie agreed. Gossip clearly was more trouble than it was worth.

"As it says in the Bible," said Fred, who liked to memorize things, "'The tongue also is a fire.'"

"What's that supposed to mean?" said Sister.

"Just that gossiping is like playing with fire," said Fred. "You can get burnt."

"I think a game of baseball would be a lot more fun than gossip," said Brother.

"Yeah," said Sister. "Let's play!"

"I'll bet me and Fred can beat the three of you, put together," said Brother.

"You're on!" said Sister.
"Play ball!" called Fred.

Sister and her friends won.
After all, it was three against two.

Activities and Questions from Brother and Sister Bear

Talk about it:

1. Have you ever heard someone gossiping or talking about someone else? Have you ever gossiped about someone else? How did that make you feel?

2. What made Sister uncomfortable when she thought about what she had said about her friend Anna?

3. Why is gossiping wrong? If you have some news about someone that you would like to talk about, what are some options besides gossip?

4. Is it ever OK to talk about other people?

Get out and do it:

1. Be positive! Be careful what you say about others. Cut out about 20 construction-paper bees and cover a jar with brown paper to look like a hive. For one week, every time you feel like talking about someone in a gossipy way, take a bee, write a good thing about that person on it, and place it in the jar!

2. As a family, talk about someone that needs your prayers and good thoughts ... that is a good kind of "talking about someone." Then, as a family, pray together for that person, asking for God to guide and bless him.

The Berenstain Bears®

Show Some Respect

written by
Jan and Mike Berenstain

ZONDERVAN.com/
AUTHORTRACKER
follow your favorite authors

It was a beautiful summer morning and the Bear family was going on a picnic. Mama and Papa packed up the picnic things. Brother, Sister, and Honey were very excited. Grizzly Gramps and Gran were coming too.

"I made a pot of my special wilderness stew for the picnic," said Gran.
"Mmm-mmm!" said Gramps. "Wilderness stew—my favorite!"
"Yuck-o!" muttered Brother. "Wilderness stew—not one of my favorites."

Sister laughed.

"What was that, Brother?" asked Mama.

"Oh, nothing, Mama," said Brother. "Come on, Sis. Let's pick out a good picnic spot."

The family headed down the sunny dirt road
to find the perfect spot for their picnic. Sister and
Brother ran on ahead.

"Wait for us please, cubs," said Mama. But Sister
and Brother paid no attention.

"Hmmm ...," said Mama, none too pleased.

"I remember a good picnic spot right in these trees," said Papa. "We used to come here when I was in school."

"That was about a hundred years ago," said Sister. "It's pretty run down now. Let's find a better spot." "Hmmm!" said Papa, none too pleased.

"I know a lovely spot down by that pond," said Mama. "Papa and I came here on our first date."

"That was an awful long time ago," said Brother. "It's full of mosquitoes now. Let's find a better spot."

"Hmmm!" said Mama and Papa, none too pleased.

"I recall a time when Gramps and I had a nice picnic on top of Big Bear Hill," said Gran as they went on their way. "There was a lovely view, and ..."

"Now, Gran," interrupted Mama. "We don't want to climb all the way up Big Bear Hill. Let's find a better spot."
"Hmmm!" said Gran, none too pleased.

The Bear family trudged across the countryside. They were getting hungry, hot, and tired.

"I have a good idea for a picnic spot," said Gramps. "How about we all ..."

"Now, Gramps," interrupted Papa. "We don't need any help—we know what we're doing."

Gramps stopped short.

"Now, just a doggone minute!" he said. "It seems to me that you folks aren't showing much respect for your elders."

"That's right," agreed Gran. "Brother and Sister are being disrespectful to Mama and Papa."

"And Mama and Papa are being disrespectful to you and me," added Gramps. "You know, us old folks know a thing or two. As the Bible says, 'Age should speak; advanced years should teach wisdom.'"

"But, Gramps!" said Papa.

"But me no 'buts,' sonny!" said Gramps. "'A wise son heeds his father's instruction,'" he added, quoting the Bible, again.

"Sonny?" said Brother and Sister. It never occurred to them that Papa was someone's "sonny."

When they thought it over, Brother, Sister, Mama, and Papa realized that Gramps and Gran were right. They were being disrespectful.

"We're sorry!" said Brother and Sister. "We were excited about the picnic and forgot our manners. We'll be sure to show more respect from now on."

"And we're sorry too!" said Mama and Papa. "We know we shouldn't speak to our elders that way."

"That's fine," smiled Gran. "All is forgiven. Now come along. Gramps will pick a good picnic-spot for us. He's Bear Country's foremost picnic-spot picker-outer."

"Yes, indeedy," said Gramps. "Besides, if we leave it up to all of you, we might starve!"

"Where are we going, Gramps?" asked Brother and Sister as Gramps led them across the countryside. "Never fear," said Gramps. "Grizzly Gramps, the picnic-spot picker-outer, is here!"

They marched over hill and dale, through wood and field.
"Now there's the perfect picnic spot!" said Gramps, at last.
"But, Gramps!" said Sister. "That's your own house."

"That's right, young'un," he smiled. "Didn't you ever hear of a backyard picnic?"

Gramps and Papa got the grill fired up and they added honey grilled salmon to Gran's wilderness stew.

"Mmm-mmm!" said Brother and Sister. "Honey grilled salmon—that's our favorite!"

They raised glasses of lemonade to Grizzly Gramps, the eldest member of the family.

"To Grizzly Gramps," said Papa, "Bear Country's best picnic-spot picker-outer!"

"You know," said Gramps, as he dug into a big helping of wilderness stew, "it's about time I got a little respect around here."